Starstruck

Starstruck

Adapted by Robin Wasserman

Based on "The Pink Guitar" and "The Little Sister"
Teleplays by Nahnatchka Khan and Madellaine Paxson

Based on *Unfabulous* created by Sue Rose

SCHOLASTIC INC.

New York   Toronto   London   Auckland   Sydney
Mexico City   New Delhi   Hong Kong   Buenos Aires

12 11 10 9 8 7 6 5 4 3 2 1   6 7 8 9 10/0

Printed in the U.S.A.
First printing, January 2006

Unfabulous

Starstruck

Have you ever felt like you were totally invisible? Like people stare right through you as if you weren't even there?

There are some people in this world who seem to have a big flashing arrow over their head, so that everywhere they go, the whole world turns to watch. Something about them just says: *Look at me. I'm exciting. I'm important. I matter*. And then there's me. The invisible Addie Singer. No flashing arrow. No one turning to watch. And no matter what I do, it seems like something about me just says: *Don't mind me. I'm not even here.*

Being invisible, that's my nightmare. No, really — it's this freaky nightmare I keep having. I'm in my favorite juice bar, *Juice!,* and I'm waiting around for my order to be ready. There's a huge crowd of people wandering around, waiting, chatting with one another — and totally ignoring me. (At this point in the dream, someone always steps on my foot — I *hate* that.) That's when Ben steps up to the mic. He's my big brother, and he works at *Juice!* in real life, too.

"Order number seventeen," Ben announces. (It's always seventeen in this dream. Don't ask me why.)

That's me! So I push my way to the front, even though no one in the crowd even notices I'm there.

"Right here," I say. "Number seventeen."

But Ben just ignores me and keeps scanning the crowd. I mean, can you believe that Ben, my own *brother*, doesn't notice me? (And it's not like that doesn't happen in the real world, too.)

"Whoo-hoo, number seventeen," I say louder. "Right here!"

"Last call for number seventeen," Ben warns. "Then I'm dumping it in the trash."

So I jump up and down, I wave my arms around, right in his face. But he doesn't see me. That's the thing about this dream. No matter what I do, or how loud I yell, people just don't see me.

"Hey! I'm *right here!*" I finally yell at the top of my lungs.

And you know what happens? Each and every time?

Ben shrugs and tosses the smoothie — *my* smoothie — over his shoulder. He grabs the next order and announces, "Order number eighteen."

That's when my best friend Geena walks right up to the counter with her receipt. (She's usually wearing a bathrobe and swimming goggles, and holding a beach ball, but I've never been able to figure out why.) Ben sees her immediately, of course, and hands over her smoothie. With a smile.

And what do I get? An earful of honking horn from the random clown who always sneaks up on me, right before I wake up.

I hate that dream.

Especially the clown.

Of course, the best part about a bad dream is that eventually you wake up. Take the last time I had my *Juice!* nightmare, for example. I woke up that morning feeling totally transparent, like the whole world was looking right through me. But a few hours later I was down in my basement, hanging out with Geena and Zach, two people I know will *always* pay attention to me. After all, isn't that what best friends are for?

It was just a typical afternoon — we were on the couch, eating popcorn and watching bad TV. In case you didn't know, when you're in a stinky mood, there's one thing guaranteed to make you feel better — watching bad TV and making fun of the shows. Trust me: the lamer, the better.

"I can't believe that girl is eating a bowl of cockroaches," I giggled, offering Geena some of my popcorn.

"I know!" Geena agreed. "I can't even choke down broccoli."

We were watching one of those lame shows where people do incredibly disgusting things, just so they can get on TV. Or at least we *were*, until Zach changed the channel.

"Ooh, *Inside the Band*!" Geena squealed as a bunch of guys with torn shirts and Mohawks popped up on the screen. Two of them were having a pretend sword fight with their electric guitars. "I love this show!"

". . . how they turned their county fair debut into a six-figure album deal," the narrator was announcing, over a bunch of shots of the band and a crowd of screaming fans. "When *Inside the Band* continues, 'River of Sick' goes from podunk to slam dunk."

"How cool would it be to be famous?" Geena asked. She was probably imagining her future as a famous fashion designer, when everyone who was anyone would be wearing a Geena Fabiano original. "To have everyone in the world know your name." She sighed in envy.

"Everywhere you go, everyone would know who you were," I said, suddenly realizing the possibilities. No more invisibility. No more fading into the wallpaper. I bet when you were famous, no one would ever throw away your smoothie.

"It depends what you'd be famous for," Zach pointed out. He's not so into the whole glitz and glamour thing — he's more into saving the world and, you know, that whole helping-people thing. "There's good fame, like saving the tree frogs. And then there's bad fame . . . like not saving the tree frogs."

Okay, so he's into helping people — and *frogs*.

Uh-oh. Huge problem. We were out of popcorn.

"Only kernels left," I announced, shaking the empty bowl in their faces.

Someone would have to drag themselves off the couch, traipse upstairs, and pop more popcorn. It's a dirty job — but someone has to do it. Lucky for us, we've been friends a long time, so we have a system.

Without a word, we each held up a fist. Odds or evens — loser sacrifices his or her spot on the couch and satisfies our junk-food craving.

"One, two, three . . . shoot!" I called. Geena and I each threw even, and Zach threw odd. Too bad, Zach. He muttered and grumbled, but he got up off the couch. Rules are rules, after all.

"Fine," Zach groused. "But I'm using non-dairy soy butter."

As we waited for Zach to come back with some deliciously fluffy new popcorn, Geena and I flipped through more of the channels. (And we both silently hoped that he was bluffing about the non-dairy soy butter. Seriously — gross.) But we weren't paying much attention to the TV. After seeing *Inside the Band*, we were both stuck inside our own heads — the idea of all that fame and fortune had given us plenty to think about.

"Tree frog," Geena mused. "Maybe I can use that as my logo. You know, when I become a famous fashion designer."

I nodded, but I have to admit, I wasn't really listening. I was too busy imagining myself as an international superstar — photographers following me around all the time, fans clamoring for my attention, all the smoothies I could ever want. . . . Imagine all the ways being famous could improve your life! In fact, when you think about it, being famous is like the opposite of being invisible. For example, if you were famous, you'd never get picked last

for volleyball. And I *always* get picked last fo
Even when it's just between me and Roger th
and *he's* the school mascot!

If you were famous, your mother wouldn't turn off the lights when you were still in the basement. I mean, there I am, sitting on the floor doing my homework. Could I be any more of a dutiful, diligent daughter — working hard, being quiet — and what's my reward? My mother finishes her book, goes up the stairs, and turns the lights off — totally forgetting I'm still down there! I get stuck sitting on the floor in the dark — and bumping my head into the wall when I blindly search for the light switch. Every single time!

And if you were famous, I'm pretty sure that your classmates would notice your feet under the stall when you were in the school bathroom. And ... well ... let's just say that maybe if you were famous, life could be a *lot* less embarrassing.

"If anyone could be famous right now, it's you," Geena suddenly pointed out. "You're a really good guitar player. You just need to play in front of people instead of alone in your room."

At first, I thought Geena was crazy. Me? A famous rock star?

But then I stopped myself — maybe I was just

being too negative. After all, I play the guitar all the time, and even write my own songs. I love it. I'd just never thought of doing it in front of other people. I mean, I play for my family sometimes and for Geena and Zach. But to play in front of strangers? Like, on a stage? With lights, and cameras, and . . . hundreds of adoring fans?

You know, it wasn't the worst idea in the world — and in fact, I suddenly couldn't believe that I had never thought of it before. Picture it: Addie Singer, live onstage. Glitter in my hair, my amp turned up as loud as it could go, a million screaming fans watching me on the jumbo screen over my head, just waiting for me to rock their world . . .

"Hey, check it out!" Geena said, pointing toward the TV. For the moment, all thoughts of fame and fortune flew out of my head. Geena had found one of those fabulous *Where Are They Now?* shows. We grinned at each other and fell silent — we love those shows, because it's so great to see how lame stars of the past turn into lamer stars of the future.

"So that's what the 'Lay off my pudding!' lady is doing now," the host was explaining, pointing toward a photo of the woman from some old pudding commercial. Then the image on the screen changed, replacing the pudding photo with the familiar logo of Huggable Diapers.

"Our next *Where Are They Now?* famous commercial is for Huggable Diapers. Let's take a look."

They rolled a clip of one of those old Huggable Diapers commercials everyone used to love. There are a bunch of grown-ups sitting around a dinner table in their fancy dining room, talking about boring stuff like mutual funds and eating boring stuff like casserole. That's when the Huggable Diapers baby shows up. He's this adorable little toddler, actually, and he wanders into the room holding up his dirty diaper.

"I went poopie!" he says proudly, and then all the grown-ups burst into laughter.

"It's the 'I went poopie' baby," the narrator explained, "a little fella named Z. C. Schwartz. If anyone knows the whereabouts of Z.C., please contact the show —"

BAM!

CRASH!

SIZZLE!

Geena and I shrieked as the popcorn bowl went flying across the room and slammed into the TV screen. The TV circuits started fizzing and crackling, and the screen went to static. Geena and I whirled around to see Zach, a little red in the face, trying to look totally casual.

"Oops," he said, as if he'd just sneezed on me

or something, rather than *broken my TV.* "The bowl . . . slipped."

"Across the room into the TV?" Geena asked, arching an eyebrow.

There was a long pause as we all stared at one another. Zach cracked first. Good thing he's not a spy — he's *never* been able to keep a secret. All you need to do is look at him funny and he spills his guts.

"All right, it was me!" he yelled.

Um, duh? Did we not just *see* the bowl go flying across the room? Who else would it be, a ghost?

"Uh, yeah, we know," I pointed out. "You're gonna tell my dad that you're the one who broke the TV."

"No, it was me in that commercial!" Zach explained, hiding his face in shame. "*I'm* the poopie diaper baby. I was a . . . child actor."

Okay, forget what I said about Zach not being able to keep a secret. He'd kept this one for years, and it was huge! Z. C. Schwartz the poopie diaper baby was Zach Carter-Schwartz, our best friend! Shocking! Amazing! And . . . the most hilarious thing Geena and I had ever heard.

"It's not funny!" he protested as we burst into insane laughter. He was trying to sound serious. But how was I supposed to take him seriously when I kept picturing him wandering into that dining room carrying his poopie diaper? "I was a spokesbaby for corporate commercialism," Zach complained. "As soon as I was old enough to realize, I gave it up and made my parents give all the money I'd made to charity."

That was enough to make Geena stop laughing. Instantly.

"What?" she asked, looking horrified.

"You gotta promise not to tell anyone," Zach begged.

But Geena barely heard him. "You gave away *all* the money?" She looked ready to leap over the couch and shake him until he admitted he was joking.

"Don't worry, Z.C.," I assured him, trying to get my giggles under control. Not that it was working. "Your secret's safe with us. Right, Geena?"

"You didn't keep *any* of it?" Geena asked again, still fixated on what that diaper cash could have done for her next shopping spree. "Like, not even enough for us to buy a necklace with a diamond charm in the shape of a '*G*'?" She sighed. Zach had just flushed her dreams of a "bling bling" life right down the toilet, along with his poopie diaper.

Um, would you think I was a bad friend if I admitted that I'm *still* laughing?

I thought about that TV show a lot the next day. So did Geena.

"We could have bought a pony," Geena mourned as we stood in line at *Juice!*

Okay, so Geena was still thinking about *Where Are They Now?* and Zach's lifestyle of the formerly rich and famous. *I* was still stuck on *Inside the Band.* I'd forgotten about it in all the diaper excitement, but when I went to bed last night, the image of that band came floating back into my mind. The band, that is — and all their screaming fans. I mean, if anyone needed to be famous and not invisible, it was me.

As I approached the counter, the crowd waited expectantly, tracking my every move.

Ben leaned into the microphone.

"And the Straw-Nana smoothie for Most Famous Rock Star on the Planet goes to... Addie Singer!" he announced.

Flashbulbs popped and the crowd burst into applause. They liked me, they really liked me! I waved and blew some kisses at my adoring fans, then leaned forward into the mic to give my acceptance speech.

"Ohmigosh!" I cried, overwhelmed. I could barely

hear myself — the whole crowd was chantin
"Ohmigosh, I can't believe it!"

"Addie, hello?" Ben, looking bored and ~~~~ ~~~,
snapped his fingers in my face. Oh, right. Back to reality.
"What do you want?"

What did I want? Simple, really. Fame, success,
rock-and-roll superstardom. You know, the basics.

Sadly, those aren't on the menu at *Juice!*

"Um, a Straw-Nana smoothie," I stuttered. And
then — why not? I smiled up at my brother and leaned
into the mic. "Thank you. Thank all of you for making this
possible."

Still half lost in my daydreams, I wandered over to
join Geena, who was reading through all the ads and fly-
ers stuck up on the *Juice!* bulletin board.

"'For sale,'" she read aloud, chuckling. "'One toilet, slightly used.' Ew."

"'Learn to speak Elvish as heard in *Lord of the
Rings*,'" I read. Unbelievable. Who posted these things?

I was about to find out.

"Check it out!" Geena yelped. She grabbed my
arm and pointed up at a pink flyer in the center of the
bulletin board. It had the word *CUTE* written across it in
giant, bright pink letters.

"'Are you CUTE material?'" Geena read. "'All-girl band seeks guitarist. Auditions tomorrow after school at St. Agnes Academy.'" We faced each other, wide-eyed, two minds with a single thought. "Addie, this is your chance to become famous!"

"Really? You think so?" But she didn't need to answer. I was totally thinking the same thing. It was fate, me coming to *Juice!* and seeing this poster. It was like I had finally found my destiny. I was nervous, and excited, and . . . really thirsty.

"Hey, that guy was behind me," I complained, suddenly noticing that everyone in *Juice!* had a smoothie in their hand, except me. "Where's my Straw-nana smoothie?" I asked the guy behind the counter.

He checked his order list. "I don't see anything here. Are you sure you ordered it?"

Forgotten again. It was a dream come true.

That night, I couldn't forget what had happened in *Juice!* — and I couldn't forget the notice that Geena and I had seen there on the bulletin board. Was it possible? Would being in a band solve all of my problems? And, more to the point, did I have the nerve to audition?

So many thoughts were cramming themselves into my head that I couldn't see anything clearly, and when that happens, there's only one sure way of figuring anything out. I hopped on my bed and grabbed my guitar and began to play.

Somehow, the music just makes everything clearer.

I hate feeling invisible.

'Cause it's miserable.

I want to be seen.

My dog, Nancy, watched me as I sang in front of the mirror with those big, sympathetic eyes of hers. I knew *she'd* never ignore me. (After all, I'm the one who feeds her.) As I kept singing and playing, all my fears and doubts began to slip away. And I knew exactly what I had to do.

Maybe getting up on stage is a chance that shouldn't be missed.

Maybe if I'm in a band, everyone will know that I exist!

While I was busy trying to make a name for myself, Zach — aka the poopie diaper baby — was wishing that he had changed his a long time ago. His day had started out like most days at Rocky Road Middle School: He was wearing his favorite alfalfa pants (yes, I have a best friend who wears pants made out of sprouts), his history quiz had been canceled, and he had basketball practice to look forward to, which was always the best part of the day. Everything *seemed* perfectly normal.

"Godzilla would beat Superman in a fight, easy," Zach argued as he and his friend Mario headed for their lockers.

"Okay," Mario conceded. "How about Godzilla versus Coach Pearson?"

"Coach Pearson, totally," Zach claimed, tossing

some books into his locker. "Godzilla's no match for Coach — have you seen the way that vein on his fore-head bulges when he gets mad?"

"You're right. That dude's dangerous."

"Great, see you at practice, man," Zach said as Mario slammed his locker shut and headed off to class.

Zach shut his own locker — and jumped back as Eli Pataki suddenly popped out from behind a door.

"Oh. Gosh," Zach said. He didn't sound too happy to see Eli — and let's be honest, no one ever is. Eli Pataki likes to think of himself as the eyes and ears of Rocky Road's principal, Principal Brandywine. He's a kid, just like us, except for the fact that he's always happy to report on whatever we're doing. Officially, Eli is the principal's assistant — unofficially, he's her spy. And he would be the first one to admit it. His favorite activity is getting other people in trouble.

"Hello, Zach," Eli said, looking very happy with himself. And when Eli's happy, you know it's time to worry. "Or should I say . . . Z.C.?"

Eli held up a videotape, and Zach's face crum-bled. He knew what was on there, even before Eli said anything.

"That's right!" Eli crowed, laughing maniacally. "I know all about your past!"

"*Shh!*" Zach urged. He leaned in close and lowered his voice to a desperate whisper. "Keep quiet."

"You think my voice is loud now?" Eli asked. "Wait until you hear it amplified during morning announcements."

Zach sighed, deciding it would be faster and easier to just give in. "All right — what do you want?"

"What any kid wants," Eli told him. "A personal assistant."

As if we needed further confirmation that Eli Pataki is *not* like any other kid.

"A personal assistant?" Zach asked suspiciously.

"Yeah, you know, like all the celebrities have. A butler." He looked down his nose at Zach, giving him his best haughty celebrity glare. "I shall call you . . . Buttington."

"Wait, you're comparing yourself to a celebrity?" Zach asked, incredulous.

"That's right."

There was a long pause, and then Zach burst into laughter. "A celebrity!" he roared, throwing his head back and laughing so loud that kids stopped in the halls and stared. "You wish!"

Eli didn't even crack a smile.

"Laugh it up, poopie," he said calmly.

Zach's laughter stopped immediately. His face fell. His shoulders slumped. And he closed his eyes, accepting his fate.

Eli Pataki, meet your new personal assistant: Zach Carter-Schwartz-*Buttington*.

Back at home, my brother, Ben, was facing problems of his own. He'd just come home from a long, hard day of school and working at *Juice!* Totally worn out, he stumbled down to the basement and flopped himself onto the couch. He was talking to his girlfriend, Tara, on the phone. Big surprise. Ever since Tara moved to California, she and Ben have been joined at the ear. He's on the phone *all* the time — everywhere I look, there's Ben, telling Tara how much he likes her, how much he misses her, how much he wishes she could see in person how totally great he is.

"Tara, work was crazy today," Ben complained into the phone. "Someone knocked the tip jar into the blender, and people refused to pay for their drinks 'cause there were pennies in them. And a few dimes. And a button. Anyway, I just wanna sit back and unwind in front of the TV —"

That's when Ben saw it. His eyes bugged out of his head and he almost dropped the cell phone. He managed to keep his grip, but he couldn't say anything — he simply screamed.

By the time he got himself together and raced upstairs, he'd found his words. Plenty of them.

"Why didn't anyone tell me the downstairs TV was broken?" Ben asked, once he'd found our parents in the kitchen. He looked the same way he did the day Dad accidentally ran over his bike. Wild-eyed and heartbroken.

"Oh, I'm sorry, Ben," Mom said, but you could tell by her grin that she didn't mean it. "I know how you like to be kept up to date on all the household appliances. FYI, the toaster is on its last leg."

"I took it in this morning," Dad explained. "It'll be fixed in a few days."

"A few *days?*" Ben gasped. It was a good thing he didn't know that Zach was the one who broke the TV. Zach had enough problems with his poopie diaper secret. "But what am I supposed to do to unwind?"

"Well, you could watch the TV in here," Dad suggested.

Parents. Sometimes they just don't understand. Ben did his best to enlighten him.

"Father," he began, sorrowfully shaking his head. "It's not just about TV watching. It's about unwinding." He got a dreamy look in his eye. "I've spent the past four years perfecting the downstairs viewing area. The distance from the couch to remote, the pillow softness, the TV angle. I can't unwind in the" — he looked around himself with disdain, as if picturing what it might be like to watch TV surrounded by the gurgling garbage disposal, our humming refrigerator, a bubbling pot of stew, and the clanging of the dishes in the sink — "kitchen."

"You could read," Mom suggested, "or take up a hobby. Spend the time bettering yourself."

"That's a good idea," Dad chimed in. "Y'know, girls really dig guys who are well rounded."

"Dad, you say that every time you want me to do something. Last week you said girls like guys who take out the trash."

It's true. And you know the best part? Ben believed him!

Okay, so back to the star of our story — by which I mean, me. Just kidding. After a long night of tossing and turning, I had finally decided to audition for the band. So after school, I walked over to St. Agnes Academy, ready to show the girls of CUTE that I had what it took to play in their band. I was totally nervous — like, instead of butterflies in my stomach, it felt like I had turbocharged fighter planes zooming around in there. But I didn't care.

I was going to go through with it no matter what. Why not? I mean, I couldn't become any *less* famous, right?

After an eternity of waiting around in the lobby, a cute, preppy girl in a Catholic school uniform finally called my name and brought me back into one of the classrooms. It was a big empty room with a long table against the back wall. Two other girls, dressed just like the first one, were sitting there watching me. It didn't take a genius to figure out that this was the band. I put on my best, brightest smile and waited for them to tell me what to do.

"That's Molly, that's Skye, and I'm Jolene," the first girl said, her voice high and flighty as if she'd just sucked the air out of a helium balloon. They were wearing matching uniforms — and matching smiles. I started to feel a little better. Maybe this wouldn't be *so* bad. "We're the *C, U, T* of CUTE, and we're looking for our *E.*"

"So now you're, like, CUT," I pointed out. My philosophy is: When in doubt, make a joke.

But the girls just looked at me in silence.

"What?" Skye asked, crinkling her face in confusion.

"You know, because the *C, U,* and . . ." I decided maybe it would be better to just give up and get on with the audition. "Never mind." I began to open up my guitar case, when Jolene stopped me with an alarmed look.

"What're you doing?"

Uh, wasn't it obvious?

"I'm . . . getting my guitar so I can play you a song for my audition," I explained, hoping it didn't sound too much like a question. Could they tell that I had never been on an audition before and clearly had no idea what I was doing?

"Oh, that won't be necessary," Skye said, and my heart sank. They'd taken one look and decided I wasn't even worth listening to?

"We just want to see how you look with one of these," Skye continued — and suddenly, things were looking up. I mean, waaaaay up. Because Skye pulled out this totally awesome pink guitar. And handed it to me!

"Whoa," I gasped, strapping on the guitar. In my ears, I could already hear the distant applause of all those screaming fans. "This is so cool!"

"Aaaand, put this on for us," Jolene requested, handing me one of those microphone headsets that all the really huge superstars wear at their concerts.

I slipped it on, feeling totally professional and ready to shoot my first music video at any moment. The

CUTE girls whispered to themselves and scribbled something down on a notepad. I just stood there, taking deep breaths and trying to remember the song I had rehearsed. I definitely didn't want to mess up my audition — these girls were obviously excited about CUTE. And I wanted *in.*

"Congratulations!" Skye suddenly said, looking up with a perky grin. "You're in the band!"

They all clapped — and they didn't *look* like they were making a joke. But . . . I hadn't even played a note.

"Really?" I asked, afraid to believe them. "That's it? I'm in?"

"We've got a good feeling about you," Jolene confirmed.

I barely heard her — I was imagining myself standing center stage, pink guitar in hand, hordes of fans beneath me. Lit up against the darkness by a single spotlight, I would raise my fist in the air, the universal symbol of rock-and-roll awesomeness. And then I would begin to play —

A high-pitched giggle wound its way into my fantasy and snapped me back to reality.

"CUT!" Molly laughed, nodding eagerly at the other girls, who clearly had no idea what she was talking about. "I just got it! That's funny! She's funny."

Okay . . . so they weren't the sharpest tacks in the box. But did it really matter? The important thing was, I was in a band. I had to keep repeating it to myself over and over, because I could hardly believe it.

I, Addie Singer, was in a band.

Good-bye, invisibility — hello, superstardom!

"Can you believe it?" I asked Geena as we stopped by our lockers before lunch. "I'm in a band!" It was about the hundredth time I'd told her my news, but Geena was just as excited as she'd been when I called her the night before.

"I totally knew you could do it," she said, also for the hundredth time.

"We have to start rehearsing right away," I explained. "Our first gig is at *Juice!*'s Open Mic night." *Our first gig* — I loved the sound of that. It was so professional, so filled with possibility — and it meant that everyone would be looking at me. no way could I be invisible if I were standing up on stage surrounded by *my band*!

As we shut our lockers, Maris Bingham and Cranberry St. Claire came parading down the hall. Most kids just "walk" — not Maris and Cranberry. They stride. They prance. They strut. And *everyone* turns to watch.

I was expecting them to pass by without acknowledging us, as usual. After all, Maris and Cranberry think they rule this school — and in their eyes, Geena and I are . . . well, nobodies.

But I'd forgotten one important thing — I was invisible no more!

"Addie, we heard you're in some band that'll be playing at *Juice!*" Cranberry said, stopping when she saw us. A couple of sixth graders who were scurrying behind her stopped, too. They crouched down behind Maris and Cranberry, holding big cameras and looking scared. Which is understandable — you'd be scared, too, if you had to spend the day with Maris and Cranberry.

"Yeah," I said. "CUTE."

"Thanks!" Cranberry spun around, giving me a full 360-view of her outfit. I decided not to explain that "CUTE" was actually the name of the band. Why bother?

"Cranberry and I wanted you to know that we'll be playing at Open Mic Night, too," Maris informed me, her nose stuck firmly in the air. Maris only knows one way of looking at people, and that's down at them.

"You guys are in a band?" Geena asked. We looked at each other in surprise — the two princesses of Rocky

Road Middle School didn't really seem like the rock-and-roll type.

"Did I say we were in a band?" Maris asked Cranberry, looking disgusted, as if we'd just suggested that she wore burlap sacks to school.

"No, you did not," Cranberry assured her.

Just then the sixth graders began snapping pictures of Maris and Cranberry and nearly blinding us all with their flashbulbs. Maris and Cranberry posed like they were walking the red carpet at a movie premiere. Despite my better judgment, I had to ask.

"Um, who are they?"

"Our entourage," Cranberry replied, as if it should have been obvious. "We thought we'd start practicing for when we become famous."

I didn't know what I was supposed to say to that — or, at least, I couldn't come up with anything polite enough to say out loud. But fortunately, I didn't have to come up with anything, because just then, Eli Pataki came over to say hello . . . and to introduce us to his new personal assistant.

"Ladies," he said gallantly. "I believe you know my assistant, Buttington." He gestured toward Zach, who was standing next to Eli, holding an umbrella over his head.

"Zach?" Geena asked. "What are you doing?"

Zach smiled at us through gritted teeth.

"I'm holding an umbrella over Eli's head. He burns easily."

"Uh, there's no sun in here," I pointed out. As if *that* was the weirdest thing about the situation.

Eli just shrugged. "Why take chances?" And with a weaselly grin, he walked off down the hall. Without another word, Zach scuttled along next to him, careful to keep the umbrella over Eli's head at all times. You know, to protect him from all that fluorescent lighting.

"I like the umbrella thing," Maris commented, cocking her head toward one of the sixth graders. "Get some."

It was an afternoon of firsts.

For me, it was my very first rehearsal with my very own band.

Desperation will do funny things to you — and without a TV, Ben was desperate. He spent about an hour sitting on the couch, staring mournfully at the empty space where the TV used to be. Maybe he was wishing it would magically reappear. Or maybe he was watching reruns in his head — with Ben, you never know. But whatever he was doing, he must have gotten bored eventually. Because by the time the CUTE girls got to my house and I led them down to the basement, there was Ben. *Reading.*

When he spotted me and the band, he grabbed the book and headed upstairs. I caught a glimpse of the title as he brushed past me — *Basic Psychology*. Great. I figured all I needed was for Ben to start analyzing me.

"TV killer," he growled as he passed by me.

"Crybaby," I shot back.

The CUTE girls watched him leave, with dreamy looks on their faces. I sighed, knowing those looks well. It's one of the painful realities of having a popular older brother — none of your friends realize what an enormous pain he can be. All they see is the good looks, the charming smile — and I get no sympathy whatsoever for having to live with Mr. Super-ego himself, Ben Singer.

"What rhymes with hottie?" Jolene gushed.

"*That* guy," Skye replied, giving Jolene a high five.

"Um, ew," I said. Sister in the room — or had they already forgotten? No way was I letting Ben make me invisible again. Not here, not to my *band.* "Okay, let's get started," I suggested, pulling out my brand-new pink guitar. I'd spent all last night practicing with it in front of the mirror — I loved the way it looked on me. Though I have to admit, I missed the familiar feel of my old guitar. Just a little.

"Oh, no, no," Jolene said, waving away the guitar. "First we have to get our dance routine locked down. As soon as Keith gets here."

Dance routine? No one had said anything about dancing — after all, I can barely walk without bumping into something or falling down. Now I was supposed to dance? And there was one issue: Who in the world was *Keith?*

"Uh, Addie?" my mom called from upstairs. "Someone named Keith is here?"

"Keith" followed my mother down the stairs. He was dressed like an MTV veejay — and he looked none too pleased with our rehearsal space, aka my basement.

"Thank you, Mrs. S," he said, handing my mom his jacket.

"Kids, can I get you anything?" my mom asked.

"Nothing for them," Keith said quickly, just as I was about to request some soda and popcorn. "I don't want anyone cramping up." He gave Mom his water bottle. "I'll take warm water, a teaspoon of sea salt, and two sprigs of parsley, thanks." He tapped his chest lightly. "I'm fighting something." Yes, Keith was a little weird — but that was probably just his artistic temperament. Weren't all creative geniuses a little kooky?

I could tell Mom was fighting something, too — the urge to throw Keith out of the house. But she knew how important this whole band thing was to me, so instead she just nodded and went back up the stairs. I breathed a sigh of relief. Keith, on the other hand, didn't even notice his close call. He placed his camera on the table and turned it on, aiming at the group.

"I am your choreographer, *not your friend*," he said sternly, pacing back and forth in front of us. "Listen to me and maybe, just maybe, you won't embarrass yourselves."

"So, when do we actually play music?" I asked.

"That sounds like a friend question," he snapped. Instead of answering, he began pointing at various spots in the room, indicating where each of the CUTE girls should stand. "You, there. You, there. You, there. And" — he gave me a suspicious look — "you, there. Come on." He clapped impatiently as we hurried into position. "Let's push aside some furniture and get funky."

I looked at Jolene, then Skye, then Molly, hoping that at least one of them shared my doubts about this whole thing. If Geena and Zach had been there, I was certain all three of us would have dissolved into giggles by now. There was something just a little *off* about this whole rehearsal. But all three CUTE girls just stared straight ahead, watching Keith and waiting for their cue.

I sighed. Guess there was nothing to do but . . . *get funky.*

Ever seen one of those music videos where the band stands in two rows and does a bunch of cheesy dance moves, all in unison? You know, pumping their fists, swinging their hips, waving their arms around as if they're directing traffic? Well, that was us — except that even after two long, hard hours of practice, we still weren't in sync.

Or at least, I wasn't.

Hey, when I signed on to be in a band, no one mentioned it was going to require coordination!

". . . and right, back, one and two, kick, three and four, turn and slide, turn, slide," Keith called out, clapping in time as the other girls followed his instructions and I tried not to bump into any of them. It was kind of hard to remember all the moves *and* try not to trip over my own feet, all at the same time.

"Turn and *strike!*" Keith shouted, our cue to stop dancing and strike a dramatic final pose. You know —

hands up in the air, knees bent, smiles bright and frozen. I know it's embarrassing — but Keith was a professional, right? So I figured he must know what he's doing.

"Better," he grunted. "Not good, but better. We'll pick this up tomorrow." He packed up his camera and abruptly turned away from us. "Bye. Great rehearsal today, CUTE girls."

Once Keith was out of there, the girls all began to gather their stuff — even though all we'd done was prance around the basement without any music. What kind of a rehearsal was that?

"Wait, that's it?" I asked, totally confused. "We haven't even played any music yet."

"Silly." Jolene laughed — a lot harder than she had at any of my actual jokes. "We don't actually *play* our instruments."

"But what about the guitar you gave me?"

"Oh, that's just for show," Skye explained cheerfully, as if I had missed the whole point. "It looks super cool. Here." She handed me a sheet of paper. "These are lyrics for our signature song."

I looked down at the page — the song was called "Cute Girls." Of course. As I read through the lyrics, if you can call them that, I began to get a very sick feeling at the pit of my stomach. The kind you get when you get to school and realize you totally forgot you have an English test first thing in the morning, and you haven't studied. The kind you get when you drink a glass of milk — and then realize the carton had expired two weeks before. Or maybe the kind you get when you realize that in a couple days, you're going to have to get up on a stage in *Juice!* and embarrass yourself in front of every single person you've ever met.

Think you want to know what the lyrics were?

Think again.

"So?" I asked finally, not really wanting to hear the answer. Geena and I were sitting at my usual table at *Juice!*, waiting for Geena to read through the "Cute Girls" lyrics and tell me if the song was really as bad as I'd thought. From the look on her face, it was worse. "What do you think of the song?"

"Uh, it doesn't really seem like you."

"Yeah, all right," I allowed, not really wanting to face up to the truth. "Maybe it's a little —"

"Fake?" Geena suggested perkily. "Heinous?"

"Commercial," I corrected her, trying to sound optimistic. "But that doesn't mean it's bad. Anyway, it's just *one* song. I gave the girls some stuff I wrote. They're meeting me here so we can go over them."

I looked around the juice bar to see if I could spot any of the CUTE girls, but all I saw was Jake Behari. Handsome, funny, popular Jake Behari. And he was headed this way!

"Hey, Addie," he said casually. Have I mentioned how cool he is?

"Jake!" I squealed. Not so cool. "Hey."

"I heard your band is performing at Open Mic Night," he said, giving me one of those gorgeous Jake Behari grins. They light up his whole face. "Can't wait to check it out."

"Cool." But it was so *not* cool. I mean, yes, cool that Jake Behari knew who I was. And that he knew I was in a band — and actually wanted to see me play. Not so cool that he was going to see it. Or hear it. Not if I had to sing *that* song. In fact, you could find these lyrics under the dictionary entry for "uncool."

As Jake Behari walked off, the CUTE girls arrived, and I resolved that I was going to be honest with them about the song — maybe I could even make them see things from my point of view.

"Hi, A," Jolene said as they all approached the table and sat down. I kept telling them that my name was Addie — but they insisted A was cuter. Or rather, CUTE-er.

"We totally don't have time to chat, we're getting our hair done before dress rehearsal."

"Hi," Geena said, holding out a hand toward Skye. "I'm —"

"Thanks, that's sweet," Skye said, cutting her off. "Listen, this is sort of a band-only meeting. But give me your e-mail and I'll put you on our fan list, m'kay?"

"Yeah. I gotta go —" Geena gave me a look like *Do you really want to waste your time with the clueless crew?* But all I could do was shrug. After all, I was a CUTE girl now. For better . . . or worse. "Somewhere else," Geena finished, and walked away.

"Bye!" Molly cried, with an enthusiastic wave. "She seems nice."

Of course she was nice, she's my best friend — which was more than I could say for the CUTE girls. But I decided to skip it and just get down to business.

"So, did you guys read the songs I wrote?" I asked.

"Yeah, we did," Jolene said, frowning. "We didn't really get them."

"Those songs weren't CUTE at *all*," Skye added.

"Why do all our songs have to be cute?" I asked, getting annoyed. I didn't write songs to make people think I was cute — I wrote them because I had something to say. Wasn't that what being in a band was supposed to be about?

The girls all gave me a patronizing look, and Molly gently put her hand on mine.

"Because," she said, slow and overenunciated as if I needed some extra help understanding her meaning. "We're *the CUTE girls.*"

Of course, silly me. What was I thinking?

At our next rehearsal, all the CUTE girls brought along their instruments. Jolene played keyboard, Skye was on bass guitar, and Molly had an awesome electric drum kit. And of course, I had my pink guitar. Which I wasn't allowed to play. We *looked* great — and we sounded . . . silent. Instead, Keith turned on the stereo, and the "Cute Girls" song blasted out of the speakers, again and again, while we lip-synched along and practiced our dance routine.

So you *still* want to know the lyrics of the song? Seriously?

Don't say I didn't warn you:

I'm such a cute girl.
Living in a cute world.
Cute, cute, cute, cute, cute, cute, cute.

Look at my cute toes.
Look at my cute clothes.
Cute shoes, cute hair, cute, cute, cute.
You will never be...
Half as cute as me...
We're such cute girls.
Living in a cute world.
Cute, cute, cute, cute, cute!

Done throwing up yet?

No? It's okay, I can wait.

So we sang that song — I mean, we lip-synched that song — over and over again, until Keith finally decide that we'd gotten it right.

"Awesome!" he shouted, clapping enthusiastically. "Do it that way tomorrow night and you will really be on your way to pop stardom!"

"Wait, you mean we don't even sing the words, either?" I asked.

"Oh, no, no," Jolene said, horrified by the thought of it.

"It would make us overly perspire," Skye explained, "and way too winded to dance."

This was getting worse by the minute.

*   *   *

"I don't know what's wrong with me," I complained. I was lying on the couch, staring up at the ceiling, pouring my heart out to the unlikeliest person in the world: my brother, Ben. "The CUTE girls might have a shot at becoming really famous, which is what I want, right?"

Ben, who was sitting by the bed and taking notes on a yellow legal pad, tapped his pen to his chin and tried to look deep in thought. *Basic Psychology* didn't have any pictures, but Ben had decided that was definitely how a psychologist was supposed to look.

"Umm-hmmm," he murmured, nodding. "And how does that make you feel?"

I sighed. I'd been trying not to ask myself that question, because I didn't really want to face the answer.

"Like I'm a fake," I admitted. "Like I'm not being myself."

"According to *Basic Psychology*, you have a decision to make. Be a CUTE girl or be true to yourself. You say you want to be famous, but you need to ask yourself: What am I willing to sacrifice to do it?"

It was a good question. And I hadn't figured out the answer yet. I just didn't understand why I had to make the choice between being famous or being myself. It wasn't fair: Why couldn't I be both?

I didn't say anything for a long time, and Ben just

sat there, looking sympathetic. He might even have been sincere — I couldn't believe that. I mean, under other circumstances, I might have been shocked that Ben was even paying attention, much less able to give me good advice. Maybe Zach should break our TV more often.

"So you're saying that if I really —"

"Unfortunately, we have to stop here," Ben said, checking his watch. "Our time is up. But we've made real progress."

I was about to complain — after all, it's not like I was *paying* Ben for his advice, so how could my time be up? But then Mom stuck her head in the doorway, and I held my breath, just hoping that she didn't have some awful chore for me.

"Ben, it's your turn to set the table," she reminded him.

Score!

"Mom, I think you're always telling us what to do because of a lack of satisfaction with your own life," Ben speculated. I bit my lip and tried not to laugh. Mom didn't look like she was in much of a laughing mood. "You've recently reentered the workforce, you're not getting any younger —"

"Stop analyzing me, Ben!" she snapped.

"Where do you think that hostility is coming from?"

"Fine, forget it! We'll use paper plates!" Mom said, exasperated. She stalked out of the room, but we could hear her muttering to herself on her way downstairs, "Gotta get that TV fixed."

I looked at Ben with a new appreciation. He may have lost his TV — but somewhere along the way, he actually found his brain.

Addie gets an awesome pink guitar from the CUTE girls — too bad she won't be playing it anytime soon.

The CUTE girls' choreographer makes them practice nonstop till they get it right.

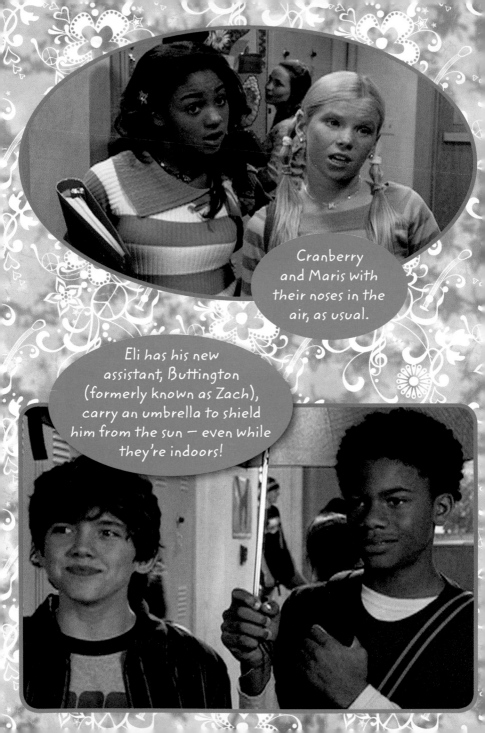

Cranberry and Maris with their noses in the air, as usual.

Eli has his new assistant, Buttington (formerly known as Zach), carry an umbrella to shield him from the sun — even while they're indoors!

"Welcome to Open Mic night at *Juice!* First up, the Principals of Song. Oh, yeah." Mario, serving as emcee for the night, ushered Principal Brandywine and two other principals onstage. They were dressed in long, elegant sequined gowns — but from where I was standing in the wings, they still looked like school principals. The audience in *Juice!* applauded politely, if not enthusiastically. It was the kind of applause you get when the audience is afraid they'll all get detention if they stay silent. And they probably would.

I looked down at myself — I was dressed in head-to-toe pink. not to mention my pink eye shadow, pink body glitter, and my hair tied up in a high ponytail with a pink ribbon. I looked like a giant puff of cotton candy. I was a CUTE girl, all right. And I was scared to death.

I tried to distract myself from my worries — and

from the painful singing principals — by spying on the audience. From my spot up on stage I could see everyone and everything. And there, over by the counter, I spotted Eli shoving a bag of dirty laundry into Zach's — um, Buttington's — hands. I couldn't hear what they were saying, but I could guess. All week long, Zach had been dusting off Eli's seat, bringing him drinks, fanning him — basically, doing whatever Eli wanted. And, of course, he was still letting Eli call him Buttington. In public. And all because Zach was afraid people would find out about his child-actor past. As Zach trudged away with the dirty laundry, I shook my head — how far was Zach willing to go to protect his image?

Then I looked down at myself again, at my bogus pink outfit and the pink guitar I wasn't allowed to play. How far was I willing to go myself?

Onstage, the principals were still going strong:

Nothing scares us, not even a parent's call,
'Cause, baby, we're queens of the hall!
A, B, C, D . . . F is for fear.
Summer school, hold you back, see you again
next year.

Suddenly, they stopped. Dead silence.

"What's wrong with you people?" Principal Brandywine cried, using the same voice she does when we're late to class. "Come on!"

At that, the crowd started applauding. I think they were just glad that the singing had stopped!

Mario jumped back on stage. "Give it up for principals Brandywine, Whitley, and Polk: the Principals of Song," Mario said with fake enthusiasm. "Next up, give mad props to . . ." He looked up from his card, as if unsure that he'd read it right. But Maris and Cranberry, who were standing on the opposite side of the stage from me, grinned brightly and nodded. So Mario shrugged and kept reading. "Give it up for The Fall Line from the House of Maris and Cranberry."

And if you can believe this, it was even worse than it sounds. . . .

The stage went dark, and the *thump-thump-thump* of techno music suddenly boomed out of the speakers and echoed through the room That's when Maris and Cranberry strutted onto the stage, dressed in their normal, everyday outfits. Not that Maris and Cranberry don't dress well — they buy all the right skirts the exact right length, every shirt a hot brand name, every belt matching their earrings and their shoes. But it's not exactly fashion-show material; it's not like they *designed* their clothes themselves. They strode back and forth across the stage carrying little dogs in their purses, doing their best catwalk impersonations — smiling haughtily down at the crowd as if they really were the country's next top supermodels. Their two sixth-grade groupies jumped up and down at the edge of the stage, snapping photos like crazed paparazzi.

Finally, after a few minutes — which felt like hours — it was over.

"Burn!" they cried in unison, and glided off stage. This was their trademark catchphrase, usually used when they'd made some nasty joke about someone — though I think the nasty joke was on them.

"Oo-kaay," Mario said slowly, his confusion mirrored in the faces of the crowd. "Thank you. Moving on. We have a few minutes until our next act, so I thought I'd fill the time by airing some dirty laundry."

I gasped — but not as loud as Eli — as Mario pulled out Eli's giant bag of dirty laundry. He snapped on a pair of yellow rubber kitchen gloves.

"Let's see," he said into the mic, opening the bag and pulling out a ratty white T-shirt. "Oh, Eli Pataki's underwear."

Zach snuck up behind me and, when I looked at

him questioningly, just gave me a silent thumbs-up. Then he gestured to me that I should turn back around and watch the stage. Good idea. Mario airing Eli's dirty underwear was something I *definitely* didn't want to miss.

"Oh, how sweet," Mario said, affecting a syrupy tone and holding up a pair of Eli's underpants. "According to the tag, these underpants come from Grandma Pataki, to be worn by her beloved 'Eli Sweetie Pie.'"

Eli, who'd already been blushing furiously, now turned bright red. He ran up on stage and started grabbing his dirty clothes from where Mario had tossed them.

"Aw, Eli Sweetie Pie, is someone cranky?" Mario asked in baby talk. "Does somebody need a nap?"

"I just need my delicates back!" Eli roared, grabbing his laundry and shuffling off stage in humiliation.

"Zach, what'd you do?" I whispered to Zach, barely able to get the words out, I was laughing so hard. "Eli will tell the whole school about your commercial!"

Zach just shrugged. "Sometimes, you gotta make a choice. And if it's a choice between the poopie diaper baby and Buttington, I'll take poopie."

Some people might have called Zach's decision crazy, or foolish. But me? I thought it was brave. He's right — sometimes you gotta make a choice.

And it was time to make mine.

*　　*　　*

"Let's give a warm *Juice!* — hey, warm juice, kinda funny — welcome to . . . CUTE!"

The audience cheered, and the stage went dark.

A hush fell over the crowd.

And then . . .

FLASH!

A spotlight flared on, and there stood Jolene, keyboard in hand, a single bright spot in the darkness.

FLASH!

Skye and her bass guitar burst into light on the other side of the stage.

FLASH!

Molly held her hand poised over her drum kit, squinting in the light.

FLASH!

An empty spot on the stage.

The CUTE girls were frozen in their dramatic poses, so they couldn't do anything but shift their eyes back and forth nervously, wondering where I was. Keith, on the other hand, was out in the audience tearing out what was left of his hair.

"She missed her cue," our choreographer said aloud, voice filled with angst. "She just missed her cue!"

I hadn't missed my cue. I'd made a choice to skip it. There was a difference. As Keith was about to find out.

Up on the stage, a loud electrified guitar chord burst from the speakers. The CUTE girls did their best to look around — without moving — to figure out where it could be coming from. They didn't have long to wonder.

Because that's when my guitar and I made our live debut.

I was still dressed in my CUTE girls costume — but, thanks to a little help from Geena, it was a little more . . . me. With a bit of quick ripping and sewing, Geena had turned my perfect pretty-in-pink uniform into something with way more punk pizzazz. Something way more rock-and-roll.

But I wasn't even thinking about what I was wearing or how I looked, or even about all the faces staring up at me in confusion and expectation. I was just thinking about the guitar in my hands and the song in my head. I was going to play the "Cute Girls" song all right — but I was going to play it with my words, my way.

I started strumming a hard, fast, and loud melody, took a deep breath, began to sing:

I can't be a fake girl living in a fake world.
Fake, fake, fake, fake, fake, fake, fake, fake.

On either side of me the CUTE girls shrugged and went into their choreographed dance routine — and inside, I smiled. If I was doing what I wanted to do, why shouldn't they do the same thing?

I write my own songs,
Even if they're all wrong.
Hey, sometimes they're sorta good.
You may not agree.
But at least they're me.
I am a real girl living in a real world.
Real, real, real, real, real, real, real.

When I stopped playing, the crowd went wild. I could see Geena and Zach in the front row cheering me on, and I even spotted Jake Behari giving me a triumphant wave. But you know what? For the first time, I didn't care. I didn't need the approval of a roomful of fans to know that I'd done what was right, and I'd done a good job. I didn't need to be a rock star — I just needed to be myself.

I left the band after that. I know — big surprise, right? The girls went back to looking for another *E*, one who would be happy being exactly the same as the *C*, *U*, and *T*. Which might be fine for someone else, but it's just not me.

And you know what? I was afraid that I'd make a huge fool out of myself at *Juice!*, but it turns out that some people appreciate the real me. Remember those two sixth graders that made up Maris and Cranberry's entourage? Well, for a while they were following *me* around. It was kind of creepy — but they did bring me sodas. And you should have seen the look on Maris's and Cranberry's faces when they figured out what was going on.

"Charles. Lawrence," Maris said curtly, the first time she came across the sixth graders bringing us a handful of sodas. "This is awkward."

"Just 'cause you stole our entourage doesn't mean you're all that," Cranberry clarified for me. Of course, only someone like Cranberry would think that a couple of sixth graders following you around would make you think you're "all that." (I guess it worked for her.) "We've had a really positive reaction to The Fall Line."

Just then, Mario came up behind Maris and Cranberry.

"Excuse me?" he asked hesitantly.

They whirled around and flashed him a brilliant smile, expecting to greet their first official fan.

"Yes?"

"Uh, you're blocking my locker," Mario said.

Let's just say that we didn't have to deal with Maris and Cranberry for a few days. And a few days is better than nothing!

"Those girls are crazy," Mario told us, as if we didn't know. "I'd take them over Godzilla and Coach Pearson *combined*."

We shut our lockers, but before we could head off to homeroom, three kids from our class wandered by and started shouting at Zach.

"What up, poopie!"

"Yo, poopie!"

"Mommy, I made a poopie!"

But Zach just smiled calmly back at them and shrugged it off. After the airing of his dirty laundry, Eli spilled the beans to everyone about Zach and his poopie diaper baby past — but the weird thing was, Zach just didn't seem to care.

"The fear of the thing is worse than the thing itself," he explained. Zach loves spouting things that are philosophical and kind of laid-back. He thinks it makes him sound deep. But in this case, I think he actually knew what he was talking about. "Plus, it was *so* worth it." He pointed across the hall toward Eli, who was cowering behind his locker as the same bunch of kids took a round of shots at *him*.

"Hey, Eli Sweetie Pie!"

"Does shmoopy doopy Shmeeli want a hug from Granny?"

"Is Eli Sweetie Pie wearing his special underpants today?"

Eli slapped his hands over his face — glaring at Zach through his fingers as we walked by.

I totally understood what Zach meant, and not just about Eli — though I have to admit it was fun to see Eli get a taste of his own medicine. But it was worth it to me, too — leaving the band. I mean, I still want to be famous. I just don't want to be fake.

Of course, after a few days, no one even remembered my big concert, and plenty of people still bumped into me in the halls and forgot my name. So until I find another way to become famous — *my way* — I might feel like I'm invisible. But you know what? Sometimes, like when I'm with Zach and Geena, I don't feel invisible at all. They're my best friends, and they *always* see me. And the best part is, they see the *real* me, and that's all they want.

Besides, there is one improvement. Now, when we

hang out in my basement watching TV, we don't have to worry anymore about who's making the popcorn. Because I know a couple sixth graders who are only too happy to take care of that.

"Addie, I can't wait until you become famous for real," Zach's always saying, usually after stuffing a wad of popcorn in his mouth. "This entourage stuff *rules.*"

Like I said, after a few days, everyone forgot about the concert, and they forgot about me, too. I decided that I could live without being world famous, at least for a while. But that didn't mean I was okay with plodding through the school day as just another face in the crowd. For some people, that might have been okay. But for me? It was a big problem — because to most people, at least the ones who even knew my name, I wasn't just Addie Singer. I was "Ben Singer's little sister."

My brother graduated from Rocky Road Middle School a couple of years ago, and *everyone* remembers him. I always feel invisible, but I don't think Ben's felt that way in his entire life. And why would he? Everyone notices him — and when they do, they never forget the experience. Ben, Ben, Ben, it's all anyone can ever talk about — how smart he is, how handsome he is, what a great leader he is, blah, blah, blah. It only takes them a couple of days after meeting me to decide I'm never going to measure up, and that's when I become "Ben's little sister" in their minds. Nothing more.

For my whole school life, I'd been searching for something that would put the name "Addie Singer" on the map. And this year, I finally achieved everything I'd hoped for. At 8:00 A.M. last Thursday morning, everyone knew my name . . . and by 8:01 I'd have given anything to be anyone *but* me.

I guess I should back up and tell you the whole story.

Like I said, everyone acts like Ben's the greatest guy to ever walk the face of the earth and I must be *so* proud to have him as my brother. It's usually the worst at the beginning of the year, when every teacher I have recognizes me as Ben Singer's little sister — that's when I get the Look. The Look says: "I expect great things from you, young lady." The Look is usually replaced with a new look a couple of weeks later — that one says: "How are *you* related to Ben Singer?"

Anyway, usually I get most of this out of the way in the first couple of weeks of school, but this year was different. It all started at the beginning of the week,

56

when Zach, Geena, and I found out that for the next four weeks, we would have to take health class instead of P.E.

"Man, I can't believe we have to sit in some boring classroom for a month instead of going to gym," Zach complained as we headed toward our first class. "I'm gonna lose my competitive edge."

"A whole month without dodgeball bruises or unflattering polyester shorts?" Geena asked incredulously. "I'm so happy I could kiss someone!"

Normally, I would have agreed with her. It's not like I enjoyed striking out in kickball or getting picked last for the volleyball team. But . . .

"I hate new classes," I reminded them.

Geena and Zach nodded sympathetically — they know all about my Ben problem. But before I could complain anymore, Principal Brandywine rolled down the hallway on her motorized scooter, heading straight for us.

"Move it, people!" she yelled as she powered down the hall, honking her horn every few seconds.

No one knows why Principal Brandywine rides around on that thing — she can walk perfectly well, but you never see her in the halls unless she's riding around on her "Li'l Scamper." Personally, I think she just likes the fact that everyone's terrified she's going to run them over.

"Ow!" a kid named Chip yelped as she ran over his foot.

"You were warned to move it," she snapped.

See what I mean?

Principal Brandywine rolled toward us, closer and closer . . . and then she was past us, rolling on down the hall.

Geena, who's usually Brandywine's favorite target, breathed a sigh of relief. "Wow. I guess Brandywine didn't notice my —"

"Fabiano!" Principal Brandywine suddenly roared, her brakes screeching as she skidded to a stop. She made an abrupt U-turn and sped down the hall right toward us, this time stopping in front of Geena.

"That blouse is much too wild and crazy," she complained, pointing accusingly at Geena's shirt, which was covered with a loud pattern of fluorescent stars and flowers. I had to admit, it was pretty bright — I had to squint to look at her. "This is an institution of learning, not the beach bungalow at a resort."

She ripped a detention slip off her pad and thrust it at Geena, looking mighty pleased with herself. After all, handing out detentions is Principal Brandywine's favorite part of the job.

Just ask Geena.

*   *   *

Poor Geena. But I didn't have much time to spare feeling sorry for her. Soon we were sitting in our very first health class, and I was too busy feeling sorry for myself.

"Dawn Ratzenburger," the health teacher announced, taking roll. I slouched down in my seat, knowing that very soon, we'd be getting to me.

"Here," Dawn chirped, raising her hand.

"Addie Singer."

"Here," I mumbled, waiting for the inevitable.

And here it came.

"Wait," the teacher said, her face lighting up. "Are you Ben Singer's little sister?"

See? I told you I hate new classes. It's always the same. My whole life, I've had to try to live up to the legend of Ben Singer. And my whole life, it's been annoying. . . .

"Aren't you Ben Singer's little sister?" my art teacher asked. "His charcoal sketch 'Still Life with Gym Sock' is hanging over my fireplace."

Frustrating . . .

"Aren't you Ben Singer's little sister? He was our best hundred-meter hurdler ever," Coach Pearson told me at the beginning of the year. Then he gave me a closer look. "But his legs weren't as skinny as yours. . . ."

And sometimes, just plain gross . . .

"Aren't you Ben Singer's little sister?" the most popular girl in the eighth-grade class asked me — it was the first time she'd acknowledged my existence. "He's so dreamy. Can you give him my e-mail?"

And now, it looked like it was going to start all over again.

"Ben was my favorite student," the health teacher babbled. "Oh, he made a fantastic model of the human heart. It pumped fake blood and everything! Wait! I think I still have it here." She began digging around in her cabinet and eventually pulled out a model of the heart that I recognized from when Ben built it on our kitchen table. I had to eat dinner on the floor for a week. "Yeah, here it is," the teacher continued eagerly. "See? You just press this, and you watch the blood go round and round and round. . . . Isn't that fantastic?"

"*That* is the most disgusting thing I've ever seen," Geena said, turning a pale shade of green as she watched the fake blood pump through the crude plastic tubes.

Suddenly the PA system dinged, and Principal Brandywine's voice boomed through the speakers. "Attention, students. As you may have heard, our class president, Randy Klein, has been injured in a toboggan-ing accident. As such, he will be unable to fulfill his presidential duties. Therefore, an election will be held next week to select a new class president — hopefully, one less accident-prone. All students who —"

There was a pause. Then a loud gasp. And then —

"My *scooter* . . ." Principal Brandywine roared in dismay, so loudly that it seemed the PA speaker might explode. *"Where's my Li'l Scamper?!"*

Somehow I got the feeling that life at Rocky Road Middle School was going to be pretty awful until the Li'l Scamper was found.

"I can't believe we spent the entire period making a 22-foot model of the small intestine," Geena complained. It was six hours later, and Geena was still whining about our endless health class that morning. "I hate health."

As we stepped into *Juice!*, hoping that some fruit smoothies would wash the taste of school out of our systems, I had to agree with Geena. Although making a model of a small intestine had been far less painful than listening to the teacher go on for an hour about the many wonders of Ben Singer.

"Hey, you!" the manager yelled as soon as he spotted us walk into the café.

Geena and I looked at each other in alarm, racking our brains for what we might have done to get in trouble at *Juice!*, of all places. At least the manager didn't have the power to give us detention.

"You!" he said again, pointing at me. "I'm short-staffed today. You want a job?"

I couldn't believe it — he'd taken one look at me and decided that I was capable of working behind the counter at *Juice!*? Just think, my very first job — and it was an awesome one. Even Ben didn't get his first job until he was sixteen. *Finally*, I would beat him at something.

"Really?" I asked, smiling modestly, even though inside I was glowing. "I'm only thirteen."

"So?" The manager grabbed my hand and dragged me toward the counter. "You're Ben's little sister. I'd clone ten Ben Singers if I could." He jerked a thumb toward the wall, where a picture of Ben was hanging under a sign that read EMPLOYEE OF THE MONTH. Of course Ben was right there adjusting the picture of himself. "But since I can't, I'll break any child-labor law to hire his little sister. So, you want the job, Angie?"

"It's Addie," I snapped, pulling out of his grip. "And no, thanks." No way was I taking Ben's hand-me-downs.

"Wow," I mused, leaning against the counter and gazing up at a picture of Ben preening. "Employee of the month."

"Yeah," Ben said, popping up from behind the counter. "Three months straight."

How is that even *possible*?!

Ben shook his head and put a hand on my shoulder, giving me a sympathetic look as if he knew exactly what I was thinking.

"Addie, Addie, Addie," he said, and it was hard to tell if he was being nice, or just making fun of me. "If you work hard, you can be almost as good as I am at everything I do."

Okay, definitely making fun of me. Big surprise.

Ben turned away and began loading up a blender with chopped fruit and juice. *Before he could put the lid on, I reached over and flipped on the blender, splattering Ben, the manager, and Ben's employee-of-the month plaque with gobs of pureed fruit . . .* in my dreams.

In reality, Ben just shot me a condescending smile and fastened the lid, while I picked up my smoothie and slunk over to Geena and Zach's table. I plopped myself down in the seat with a loud sigh.

"Addie, what's wrong?" Geena asked. At least *someone* cared.

"Ben's the employee of the month. Again. It isn't fair!" I put my head in my hands. "Everybody loves him,"

I added, in a muffled voice. "When he was in middle school, he was in every single club. He was even vice president. And me? I'm just Ben's little sister."

"Ben was *vice* president?" Geena asked, sounding shocked. "I'm surprised he wasn't president. The hottie always wins."

Suddenly, it was as if a lightbulb had clicked on over my head. I looked up at my friends, beaming. "That's it!" I cried, the plan already half formed in my head. "I'll run for class president! That's totally something that Ben never did. Oh, and you guys can help me with my campaign! You can make buttons and posters. . . ."

Geena and Zach didn't say anything, but I knew I'd just caught them off guard. Once they had some time to think about it, they'd be just as excited as I was. Because this was the perfect way to establish myself as "Addie Singer. Period."

After a few days of furious campaigning — or at least a lot of posters — Principal Brandywine called a giant assembly to announce the winner of the election. The other candidate and I stood on stage behind her, holding our breath and trying not to look nervous. As Principal Brandywine stepped up to the mic, I closed my eyes, crossed my fingers, and waited for the words I was almost convinced I would hear: "Our next class president . . . Addie Singer!"

"And now, for the results of our election for class president," Principal Brandywine began, speaking way too slowly. I couldn't stand to wait any longer. "Chip Keaton received 248 votes. Write-in candidate Clarence the Chatty Clam received 92 votes."

There were way less than 400 kids in our class. I may not be that great at math, but even I knew this wasn't going well.

"And in an embarrassing third-place finish," Principal Brandywine continued, "Addie Singer received two votes."

Two votes!

Two votes?

As soon as the assembly was over, I cornered Geena and Zach. Some campaign managers *they* turned out to be!

"Which one of you didn't vote for me?"

Giving me a sickly smile, Zach raised a finger.

"Your environmental platform was weak," he said, shrinking away from my wrath. "So I went with the third-party candidate."

"He's a *clam*!" I pointed out, my blood boiling.

Zach just shrugged. "He cares about the ocean!"

I couldn't get the election out of my head. Not just because I was totally embarrassed to have gotten only two votes, and not just because I'd lost, and lost miserably, to a fictional *clam.* Although neither of those helped much. But the worst part of all was that I had finally come up with something that Ben had never done, something that could be completely my own. And it had been a total bust.

I was right back where I'd started.

Nowhere. Nobody. Ben Singer's little sister.

"Ben, Ben, he's a man among men," I sang at the top of my lungs, strumming along on my guitar. I was safely hidden away in the privacy of my own room, so I knew no one would hear. But even if they had, I was too mad to care.

> *He's every girl's sweetheart,*
> *He's every guy's friend.*
> *He's swum in every ocean.*
> *His life has been a dream.*
> *He's loved by all mankind,*
> *HE'S ONLY FIFTEEN!*
> *There's got to be something that Ben hasn't*
>   *touched,*

Some prize his grubby hands haven't clutched.
'Cause being in his shadow is JUST TOO MUCH!

I flopped back down onto my bed and sighed in disgust.

Usually, making up a song about something helps me get it out of my system. Once I've spent some time strumming my guitar, singing my heart out, and dancing all over my room, whatever problem I'm having seems a lot clearer. Sometimes I even have the answer.

Not this time. So I decided it was time for more drastic measures.

Sneaking downstairs, I dumped out a bag of cookies and arranged them on a plate, and then crept back upstairs and quietly knocked on the door of Ben's room.

"What do you want?" he called irritably. He hates to be bothered up in his bedroom. Especially by me. I've only been in there twice in the last six months.

"I baked you some cookies," I said hopefully. (Baked, brought — what's the difference, really?)

"Leave them outside and back away slowly," Ben said suspiciously. He's always suspicious when I'm nice to him. Maybe because it doesn't happen very often.

I decided to drop the fake act and be honest. Hey, maybe it would work.

"Okay, I just wanted to see your middle school yearbook," I admitted.

"Oh — that's all?" And the door swung open. "You didn't have to go to all this trouble." He grabbed a cookie and stuffed the whole thing in his mouth. "Cash would have been fine."

I stepped over the threshold and into Ben's room, trying not to make it look like I was snooping. It was a total mess — the floor was covered in torn magazines and dirty T-shirts, and about a zillion posters of sports cars and basketball players were plastered across the wall. *This* was the room of Rocky Road Middle School's golden boy? Bizarre.

"What do you want my old yearbook for?" Ben asked, digging through a pile of junk.

"I . . . uh . . ." No way was I going to tell him the real reason. But I hadn't been clever enough to come up with a fake one ahead of time. "I just wanted . . . to see an old picture of a teacher."

Ben tapped a finger against his temple, looking impressed.

"So you can blackmail him later — smart. A class president can never be too careful."

I blushed and looked away. "Oh, I'm not class president."

"I don't understand," Ben said, looking more confused than usual. "I thought you ran."

"I did."

He stared at me blankly. Was he really going to
make me say it out loud?

"I just didn't win."

Ben burst into laughter. Nice. You know, it's not like
I was expecting a pity party, but I didn't think that my
own brother would laugh at my pain!

"Didn't win!" he chuckled. Then, suddenly catch-
ing the look on my face, he calmed himself down and
frowned. "Oh, didn't win. Oh — you're serious. Sorry.
Losing's just not something I'm familiar with."

"Can I see your yearbook or not?" I asked, trying
to keep my temper.

He finally dug it out from under a giant pile of
junk, and I plopped down on his bed, flipping through it.
Ben looked over my shoulder, smiling at all those memo-
ries of the good old days.

"Ahh, there I am." He pointed down toward the page
I had randomly opened to, and there he was, front and
center, wearing his old letter jacket. I flipped the page.

"And there . . ."

"And there . . ."

And —

"I'm not on this page," Ben said, perplexed. He looked closer. "Wait, there I am. Behind Coach Pearson. I wasn't even on this team. Coach just wanted me to be in all the pictures."

I couldn't believe it.

"You're on every page!" I mean, I always knew Ben had done a lot of stuff in middle school, but this was ridiculous. How was I ever supposed to compete?

"You can't say that yet," he countered smugly. "You haven't gotten through the whole thing. Let's continue."

He tried to flip the page, but no way was I going on a stroll down the memory lane of Ben's middle school triumphs. Instead, I started flipping through at super speed, glancing at each page just to confirm that Ben's face was staring up at me from each of them. It was.

"You were a *mathlete*?" I asked in disbelief, pausing at the last page, where Ben was smiling cheerfully amid a group of mathletes decked out with pocket protectors and calculators. Ben, of course, looked just as cool as ever.

"Do you forget who you're talking to? Mathlete is just athlete with an mmmmm."

I threw myself back against the mattress in despair.

"My picture was only in the yearbook once last year," I admitted. "And it wasn't even good."

"Don't feel bad," Ben said, and I actually sat up again to take a closer look at his face. Was he actually trying to be comforting? Supportive? Ben? "You'll at least get your name in the school paper," he continued. "You know, when they write the article about the new president, they always mention the losers."

I leafed through a thick stack of cut-out newspaper clippings from the back of the yearbook.

"I had a little press in my day," he bragged.

A little? That was the understatement of the year. There had to be a hundred articles! I flipped through them, but I didn't have the heart to do more than skim the headlines.

"These are all about you?" I couldn't believe it. "Did you write these?"

"I don't write newspaper articles," Ben assured me. "I inspire them."

"Wait a minute —" I dropped the clippings, and they scattered onto the bed and the floor, but I didn't even notice. A brilliant idea was dawning on me — and this time, it might actually work. "You don't write?" I asked again, just to make sure. Ben nodded.

That was it! The one thing Ben had never done. All I had to do was write an awesome article for the school paper. Then everyone would know my name!

"Um, hello?" The sound of Ben tapping against the empty plate woke me from my daydream — but that was okay. I was going to make it a reality. No matter what it took.

"If you're gonna stay here any longer," Ben reminded me, "I'm gonna need some more cookies."

"Well, well, well. Addie Singer. I've just finished archiving all the articles about your legendary sibling, Ben. Took. Me. Hours."

I was sitting in the cramped newspaper office facing Mary Ferry, the editor-in-chief of the paper and, by the looks of it, the one person who wasn't particularly impressed by Ben's overflowing resume. Not if it meant more work for her.

"Sorry about that," I said, shrugging. "He was kinda popular."

Mary leaned across the table and fixed me with an intense gaze. I guess she figured I came here to ask if I could write for the school paper. Actually, everything about her was kind of intense. I'd heard that Mary ran the paper with an iron fist, just counting the days until she could get out of school and into the real world and work for a real, big-city newspaper. I admired that — I didn't really have any goals beyond making it through the seventh grade without falling down too many times. And maybe getting through five minutes of conversation with Jake Behari *without* saying something stupid.

"Don't think you're getting special treatment just because you're Ben Singer's little sister," Mary warned. "His hottie factor does not influence me in the least."

I leaned forward in my chair, trying to match Mary's intensity. And on this particular issue, I was pretty intense.

"I'm not looking for special treatment," I promised. "I don't want to be known as Ben Singer's little sister. I'm trying to be my own person."

Mary nodded once, and it seemed I had passed the test.

"All right, then. I do have one opening." She held up an issue of the school paper, showing me a section labeled "My Turn."

I tried to suppress a grin — Mary didn't seem like the type who would appreciate too much smiling.

"You can write an opinion for the op-ed section of the paper called 'My Turn,'" Mary offered.

"Great! What's the topic?"

"Whatever you want." Mary looked at me like maybe she'd judged me way too quickly, and maybe I didn't deserve the opportunity after all. "It's your opinion," she pointed out. "Hence the term. Op-ed. Op-inions, and ed-itorials. Get it?"

Okay, I finally got it. Fortunately, Mary was moving too fast to even notice.

"You'll have to come up with something current and interesting. No fluff," she warned me brusquely.

This was so fabulous — not only was I going to write something for the school paper, something Ben had *never* done, but I could write anything I wanted! I would get to come up with an opinion on my own, on something *I* cared about, and share it with the entire school.

Just one little problem: What was I going to write about?

My mind was a total blank. Sure, there were issues I cared about — better food in the cafeteria, fewer boring classes and more study halls, getting rid of detention, but that was stuff everyone wanted. (It was also stuff none of us was ever going to get.) I didn't really have anything new to say on any of those subjects, nothing that would make me stand out, that would make me special. I needed something new and different, something exciting — an opinion that would set me apart from my brother's legacy, that would introduce the whole school to the unique mind of Addie Singer. But what would it possibly be?

As I was racking my brain to come up with something "current" and "interesting," the PA system dinged, and Principal Brandywine's voice blared out of the tiny speaker by Mary's desk.

"I want every single student to report to my office for scooter theft interrogation."

Mary Ferry glared at the PA speaker.

"I just know this is violating some sort of student rights," she complained. Did students even have rights? I'd never thought about anything like that before, but suddenly I realized maybe Mary was right. Maybe we did — and Principal Brandywine was scooting all over them! "President-Elect Chip isn't doing anything about it."

In the worst possible timing, Chip himself was passing by the office just as the words slipped out of Mary's mouth.

"I heard that," Chip snapped, poking his head in. "One more word outta you and I'll turn your 'office' back into a closet."

Mary opened her mouth, then closed it again without saying anything, probably figuring that the school newspaper needed the office space more than she needed an argument with Chip. Besides, Mary was right — Chip wasn't going to do anything about Brandywine's indecent investigation.

But maybe I could. . . .

After meeting with Mary, I went down to Principal Brandywine's office to check out the interrogations. I got there just in time to give Geena some moral support before her appointment with the principal — and just in time to run into Jake Behari.

"Hey, Addie," he said, giving me a casual wave as he joined the crowd of students waiting outside the principal's office.

"Hey, Jake." Inside, I smiled. I never know what to say to Jake, but at least this time, I'd gotten two words out. And they'd sounded pretty normal. Hopefully, he wouldn't notice that my face was about ten times redder than usual. Although actually, my face turned ten times redder than usual every time I saw him — so he probably thought that was my normal color.

"How's it going?" he asked. I almost didn't hear him — I was too busy looking at his dark eyelashes.

How was it going? A tricky question. Because it meant I had to come up with an actual answer. (Usually when I'm talking to Jake, I like to stick to "yes" and "no." I'm usually way too freaked out to come up with anything better than that.)

Lucky for me, before I could answer, we were interrupted by a loud shriek from Principal Brandywine's office.

"Can't... take... any... more..." a girl's voice moaned. A few seconds later, she staggered out of the office, her face crumpled, her spirit destroyed.

Eli Pataki, the principal's eager assistant, stepped out behind her. Unlike the girl, he looked fresh, energetic, and ready for more.

"Next!" he shouted, scanning his clipboard. "That's you, Fabiano."

Geena stood frozen for a moment, then began inching toward the office door. Very, very slowly.

"Be strong," I urged, patting her on the shoulder. It would all be over soon — one way or another.

Behind the door, in Principal Brandywine's inner sanctum, Eli gave Geena a sickeningly sweet smile and asked her to sit down.

"Can I offer you some gum?" he asked, holding up a pack of gum. Principal Brandywine just sat silently behind the desk. Watching.

"Chewing gum isn't allowed on school property," Geena pointed out, narrowing her eyes at Eli.

"Oooh, she's *good*," Eli admitted. He exchanged an impressed look with Principal Brandywine. They nodded sharply at each other, then Principal Brandywine leaned forward toward Geena, gazing at her the way a hawk zeroes in on its prey.

"So. It must be terrible having to waste away every afternoon in detention, huh, Miss Fabiano?" she asked. "I can understand why you'd want revenge on the individual handing out the pink slips."

But Geena wasn't going down that easily.

"Detention's actually not so bad," she said with a perky smile. "The people are nice."

"*What are you hiding?*" Principal Brandywine suddenly roared.

"Nothing!" Geena shouted.

"You took my scooter, didn't you?" The principal leaned across the desk toward Geena, ready to pounce. "I can tell by that defiant look in your eyes."

"I didn't take your scooter," Geena countered, refusing to look away from Principal Brandywine's gaze. "But I'm glad someone did. That thing's a menace to open-toed shoes."

There was a sudden, heavy silence. *No one* stood

up to Principal Brandywine like that. Especially when it came to her scooter.

Then Eli shook his head and made a check on his clipboard.

"She's clean," he affirmed.

The principal looked disappointed. But she shrugged and, with a sharp nod, dismissed her latest victim.

"You're free to go."

As Eli closed the door behind Geena, Principal Brandywine slumped back into her chair. She shook her head, totally frustrated.

"These interrogations are taking much too long," she complained, "and going nowhere."

"Principal Brandywine . . ." Eli nibbled on the edge of his lip, nervous about the suggestion he was about to make. But it had to be said. "Maybe you should just give it up. We could search every locker in this school but still not find any evidence."

Her eyes widened, and a smile broke out across her stormy face.

"Genius, Pataki! A schoolwide locker search!"

And that's how, a few hours later, Geena, Zach, and I came out of the cafeteria to discover that all of our lockers had been pried open. All of our stuff — our *personal, private* stuff — lay scattered all over the hallway. As all the students crowded at the edges of the hall, frozen in shock and horror, Principal Brandywine paced angrily back and forth, stepping all over our belongings.

"There's no evidence here," she snapped, disgusted. "Clean up this mess!"

With a small nod, the janitor pulled out a gigantic broom and began sweeping all of our bags, notebooks, magazines, and adorable, just-purchased magnetic locker mirrors away. That was it? They'd pried open our lockers, dumped out our lives for the whole school to see, and now they were just sweeping it off to the trash? I couldn't believe it!

"What about our rights?" Mary Ferry exclaimed as the janitor passed us by. "I'm certain this is in violation."

As soon as I heard her, I knew what I had to do.

"Okay, Principal Brandywine has been spending way too many hours watching cop shows on TV," Geena complained. But she shrugged her shoulders, as if there was nothing anyone could do to stop her.

"This is terrible!" I cried. But the plan was coming together in my head. After all, I watched cop shows on TV, too, and I knew that you couldn't just invade people's privacy whenever you wanted to. Well, maybe I didn't *know* — but it sounded like something people shouldn't be allowed to do. Principal Brandywine probably just figured that no one would have the nerve to call her on it. Little did she know — Addie Singer, Girl Reporter, was on the case. "Someone should really do something about this."

"We could hold a protest," Zach suggested. He loves protesting. "Or —"

"Or write a scathing article for the school paper's op-ed section!" I cut in.

"I like the protest idea better," Geena mused. "I could pick out cute outfits for us in case the news crews came."

But I just ignored her. This time, *I* was going to be the one doing the protesting. I was going to make a name for myself — I'd be a hero, a warrior for student rights. And finally, I'd be out from under Ben's giant shadow.

That night at dinner, the scooter situation was all I could talk about.

"And then all the stuff in our lockers was just dumped on the ground," I recounted for the rest of my family. "And then the janitor swept it away! I don't know what Principal Brandywine's deal is."

"Ahhh, Principal Brandywine." Ben sighed. He got

that look in his eye, the one he always gets when he's about to start talking about his golden years in middle school. I rolled my eyes in disgust, but no one noticed. My parents were too busy staring adoringly at the oh-so-fabulous Ben — and Ben was too busy looking into the past at his oh-so-fabulous self. "Back when I was at Rocky Road," he continued, "I told her I was a foreign exchange student from a war-torn country. She treated me so special after that."

My parents just chuckled — even though I knew that if *I* lied to the principal, I'd be grounded for a week.

"I forgot about that." Mom laughed. "Honestly, Ben, I don't know where you get your imagination."

"From me," Dad boasted. "Remember those short stories I wrote about the lost island of Baboo?"

Ben and I just looked at him blankly. We still remembered his stories all right — even though we'd done our best to forget them.

"Baboo was a whale," he reminded us, thinking we'd just forgotten all about his creative brilliance. "That's why it kept disappearing. Oh, not it, but he. *He*, actually, because Baboo was a male whale. But anyway."

We just kept staring at him in confused silence, hoping that eventually, he'd give up. It had worked in our childhood — and it worked now.

"Ahem." Dad pretended to clear his throat, and came back to the present. "What happened when Principal Brandywine found out the truth?"

"It was hilarious," Ben reminisced. "She was mad at first, but I said, P-Bran, you just gotta chill, man . . . learn to roll with the funnies."

"You called Principal Brandywine 'P-Bran'?" I asked in disbelief.

"Yeah. She loved it. I think it made her feel special."

Oh, *please.*

I felt like I was going to throw up — and I must have looked it, too, because Mom suddenly remembered that I was at the table.

"Addie, honey, what's the matter?" she asked.

"It's just . . . Ben's a legend at Rocky Road." The whole thing had been bouncing around in my head for so long that I just couldn't stop it from popping out. Even though I hated to admit it in front of Ben. "Even P-Bran liked him." I sighed. "I'm not even sure she knows my name."

"Please," Ben protested, totally shocked. "You have it easy. Just think how hard it was for *me!*" Yeah, right. "I had to start school a total nobody. No one there had even heard the Singer name before I walked in the door."

"I went to school at Rocky Road," Dad reminded him.

"Dad, come on." Ben shook his head and shot Dad a pitying look. "All the teachers you had are dead by now."

Dad opened his mouth to respond, but as always, Mom jumped in to save the day.

"More souvlaki?"

None for me. I'd totally lost my appetite.

I stayed up all night writing that "My Turn" article. For hours and hours, I just sat in front of my computer, staring at that blank screen with the blinking cursor. There's nothing worse than a blank page, especially when you have nothing to say. I mean, I had plenty to say — I just couldn't figure out how to get it all down on paper.

Sometimes, I just had to take a break — check my e-mail, call Geena, play with the old paddleball my brother gave me when I was eight, but then I got back to work. I *had* to come up a great idea.

Finally, late into the night, hours after everyone else had gone to bed and the world outside my window was totally silent, I got an idea. And then another one. I sat down in front of the computer, and this time, I wasn't intimidated by the blank screen. I just let my fingers fly, typing and typing as fast as I could to get all the words out. My fingers couldn't move fast enough to keep up with my brain, which was jumping from one thought to the next at lightning speed.

By the time the sun rose and the first rays of light peeked through my blinds I had fallen asleep with my head on my desk next to my computer. My dog, Nancy, was asleep next to me. And my very first article for the school paper was almost finished, and almost perfect.

In a couple of hours I would be sitting in home-room, and I would be totally zonked. Making it through the day on no sleep was going to be a nightmare. But it would be worth it.

I hoped.

The next morning, I sat on the edge of my chair in the tiny newspaper office and waited impatiently for Mary Ferry to read my article. She was taking forever. I couldn't stand the wait. I squirmed around in the chair, counted the number of cracks in the ceiling paint, and tried my best to stay awake. At least until I could hear what she thought of my work. Finally, she looked up from the article, frowning. I tried to read her expression, but it was no use — Mary Ferry is almost always frowning.

"This . . ." she began, as I took a deep, nervous breath, "is the best op-ed I've ever read."

Yes!

"But there's no way we can run this."

Uh . . . what?

In my dream world: I swept all the junk off of

Mary's desk and leaped on top of it. I grabbed her by the lapels and pulled her toward me, so her face was trapped just inches from mine. "What do you mean, you can't run it?" I hissed, my voice strangled by frustration. "I need this article!" I shook her, and she looked up at me with wild, frightened eyes. "Do you understand me, Ferry? I need it!"

In reality, I just sat there calmly. At least I looked calm on the outside. On the inside, I was about to explode.

"Brandywine has to approve everything that goes into the paper," Mary explained.

"Oh." And suddenly, I understood. I could picture the principal, sitting behind her giant desk in her giant office, leafing through each of the newspaper articles. She probably had a big stamp that said APPROVED. It was probably a big power trip for her, policing what went into the paper. And it meant no power for the rest of us.

"She's like the gatekeeper," Mary continued. "We give her everything to read, and if it's okay with her, she puts it in her 'Approved' folder. If it's *not* okay with her . . ."

Mary didn't need to say anything more. I could picture it pretty vividly. Principal Brandywine reading my article with steam blowing out of her ears. Principal Brandywine tearing my article in half while shrieking,

"Not approved!" Principal Brandywine dipping my article in a bowl of glue and layering it onto a life-size papier-mâché bust of herself — a sculpture for the next county art fair, made entirely of rejected journalism.

Okay, maybe that last part wasn't as likely. But I was certain that whatever Principal Brandywine did with my article, she wouldn't let Mary print it.

"She's never gonna approve a scathing critique of *her,*" Mary said, shuddering, and I wondered if she was envisioning the same scene I was. "You know, Addie, you should keep writing. You're really good. But if you want to be in this business, you'll have to learn to proof-read. You had a lot of typos."

She handed the article back to me. I guess I should have been happy that she liked my article, and that she thought I was good at this, but it didn't really help. All I kept hearing was "there's no way we can run this." So much for making a name for myself. So much for getting out from under Ben's shadow.

now what?

All day long, I'd been too tired to think straight — but that night, I couldn't fall asleep. I just couldn't stop thinking about my op-ed. And the fact that no matter how hard I tried, I would never be anything more than

Ben Singer's little sister. Eventually I gave up on trying to sleep. I got out of bed, turned on my light, and grabbed my guitar. I had something I needed to say — or rather, sing.

"Don't wanna be 'little sister' anymore," I sang sadly, strumming away. Nancy lay at my feet and looked up at me with her big, brown, sympathetic eyes. I knew she understood exactly what I was feeling.

> I've lived that way forever, it's a giant bore.
> Wanna make my own name,
> "Little sister" is so lame.

Suddenly, I wasn't sad anymore. I was angry. Mary had said my article was *good* — and deep down, I knew she was right. This was a really important topic, and my argument was *right,* I was certain of it. Was it fair that no one was going to read it? Was it fair that I was going to stay totally unknown, that my article would end up part of Principal Brandywine's art project, just because it said something she didn't like?

No, it wasn't fair at all. It stunk.

And I wasn't going to take it.

"Ben, he'll be so amazed," I sang, louder and faster.

I jumped up on my bed and started jumping up and down in time with the music.

Little sister's gonna show him up someday!
He'll have to learn . . .
It's gonna be my turn!
Don't wanna be "little sister" anymore.

After that, I had no trouble falling asleep. After all, I needed to be well rested for the next morning if I was going to accomplish my mission. It was time for Ben Singer's little sister to grow up.

Principal Brandywine picked up the phone on the second ring.

"Brandywine speaking."

I took a deep breath, and then did my best to make my voice sound low, scratchy, and completely unrecognizable.

"If you ever want to see your scooter again, meet me in the cafeteria right now," I ordered her.

"Who is this?"

But I'd already hung up. I snuck down the hall to the principal's office, just in time to see her rush out.

Perfect. I slipped into the office and went right to the desk, digging through a stack of papers until I found what I was looking for: the "Approved" folder. Inside were all the articles approved for publication in the school paper. And just as I'd suspected, they were each stamped with a big, red APPROVED across the top.

I found Principal Brandywine's big stamp in her top desk drawer and quickly stamped APPROVED on my own article. All I needed to do was slip it inside the folder.

I opened the folder and — stopped. I'd always been a pretty good student, never really got into any trouble. Geena was the one who got detentions all the time. Zach was the one who protested loudly for whatever he believed in. Me? I was usually just along for the ride, standing around in the background and trying not to get in trouble. Like I said before, Principal Brandywine didn't even know my name. But this was big. This could get me into a ton of trouble. And if I did it, there'd be no turning back.

On the other hand — if I didn't do it, I'd never make a real name for myself. I'd never be anything but Ben Singer's little sister. And I couldn't take that thought — so my decision was made.

I slid my article into the "Approved" folder and stuck it back on the principal's desk. Then I crept out of the office. No one would ever know I was there. Tomorrow morning's "My Turn" column would be written by Addie Singer. Everyone would know my name.

As I wandered down the hallway away from the office, trying to look casual and not guilty, I couldn't help smiling. It really was finally *my* turn.

Eight A.M., Thursday morning. The whispers started as soon as I walked in the door. As I strolled down the hallway, all the kids turned to stare at me in wonder. I could hear them asking one another, "Is it her? Is that Addie Singer?" A crowd formed, and even the teachers huddled at the fringes, pointing me out to one another. They were all so amazed by my presence, so impressed — and I knew then that *everyone* must have seen the article.

Before I got to my locker, some ninth-grade jock stepped into my path — I stopped just before bumping right into him.

"Are you Addie Singer?" he asked.

I couldn't believe word had traveled so fast. It was 8:01 A.M., and I was already famous.

"Yes. Yes, I am," I responded proudly.

He turned toward a group of his friends and beamed.

"It's her! Addie Singer!"

This fame thing was better than I'd ever imagined. No wonder Ben had such a big, fat head if this was the kind of treatment he'd been getting all his life. All the kids were looking at me with awe, they were whispering about what I'd done, they were —

Laughing in my face?

The jock guy crumpled up his newspaper and threw it at me.

"Hilarious," he said, walking off.

That's when I took a closer look at the crowd of students. Yes, they were all talking about me and pointing at me — and they were definitely laughing at me. At *me*, author of the best "My Turn" this school had ever seen!

My seventh-grade art teacher walked past me, shaking her head in disappointment.

"I expected more from Ben Singer's little sister," she said, tossing her copy of the school paper in the trash.

What was going on? How could my moment in the spotlight have gone so bad so quickly? I grabbed a copy of the paper and flipped it open to the op-ed page . . . and gasped. There it was, my article, just as I'd imagined it — except for the headline.

My Turd, *by Addie Singer.*

"I can't even say it." Mary Ferry's head suddenly popped up from behind my copy of the paper. And she looked mad. Madder than usual.

"I'm sorry," I stuttered. "I guess I forgot —"

"To proofread?"

"Yeah." I couldn't believe this was all happening to me. And I *really* couldn't believe that I'd brought it on myself. Of all the words to misspell — I had to choose the one that was printed in big, black, boldface print at the top of the article? I must have been so nervous about sneaking it into the principal's office that I hadn't even noticed it said "My Turd" instead of "My Turn." I'd embarrassed myself in public before — a lot — but I'd never done anything like this before. This was big. Huge. And it was all my fault.

"Look, I admire the audacious slipping of your editorial into Brandywine's 'Approved' file," Mary admitted, "but I can't allow you to continue writing for the paper. Neglecting to proofread is the utmost in journalistic sloppiness."

Not only had my editorial made me a laughingstock but now I'd never get the chance to write another one? I was totally crushed. And then Principal Brandywine showed up, just in time to kick me while I was down.

"Report to my office immediately, Singer!"

I guess she knew my name after all. I slouched down the hall behind her — I wasn't even afraid of what she'd do to me. After all, the whole school was already laughing at me. What punishment could be worse than that?

"This is the most reprehensible stunt ever perpetrated at this school!" Principal Brandywine had been yelling at me for ten minutes straight. I just slunk lower and lower in my seat, waiting for it to end. "We have received an unprecedented number of calls from parents threatening to move out of the district."

"I'm so sorry, Princi —" I paused, and decided maybe it was time to try to get chummy with her. "P-Bran . . . ?"

She just glared at me. A minute ago, I would have said it wasn't possible for her to get any angrier than she already was. But I'd been wrong.

"You have brought shame upon this school, shame upon our newspaper!" she continued. "And now *you* shall be shamed by receiving one week of detention."

She handed me a pink slip and I looked down at it as if my hand belonged to someone else.

"A whole week?" I couldn't believe it. I'd never even had *one* day of detention before, and now I had to go for a whole week?

Eli Pataki, who'd been lurking in the corner of the office the whole time, escorted me toward the door and pushed me through it before I could protest.

"You caught her at a bad time," he explained as he hurried me out. "She's a little grouchy since the scooter incident. I told her she should get some air, get out, but —"

"Quiet, Pataki!" Principal Brandywine snapped. She ran her hands through her hair in frustration, and then sighed. "I give up. Get started on filling out the insurance papers so I can get a new scooter."

"Principal Brandywine?"

I hesitated just on the other side of the office door, wondering what Eli was going to say next. I'd never heard him sound so nervous, so tentative.

"Perhaps it would be best if you took this opportunity to start . . . walking on your own?" he suggested.

Principal Brandywine looked up at him as if he'd just sprouted another head.

"Walking? Why would I do that?"

Eli pulled out an envelope and tossed it on her desk.

"The results of your EKG came in," he explained. "The doctor did say you should be exercising more. Maybe . . . you don't need a scooter."

"You opened my mail?" Principal Brandywine asked incredulously. "I'll have you know that's a federal offense!"

Eli turned red and backed away from her desk, worried she was about to blow. But he still tried to bluster his way out of trouble.

"As principal of this school, your health affects us all, so . . ."

Principal Brandywine suddenly leaped out of her chair and pointed an accusing finger at Eli.

"You!" she cried, lunging toward Eli. "*You* stole my Li'l Scamper!"

At that, Eli ran out of the office, almost mowing me down on his way down the hall.

"It was for your own good!" he called back over his shoulder. "You need the heart health!"

Principal Brandywine hiked up her skirt and raced out of the office, hot on Eli's trail. It was the fastest I've ever seen her go, including all those times she rolled down the hall with her scooter set on full turbo power.

"I'll show you heart health!"

I was a little nervous about my first afternoon in detention. I had no idea what to expect. I mean, who knew what kind of delinquents spent their afternoon stuck in that tiny, crowded room next to the cafeteria? Would it be like prison, I wondered, with bars on the windows and a scary guard at the doorway to keep us prisoners from making a break for it?

Uh, not so much.

The detention room was just a normal classroom, except it smelled like stale potatoes and mystery meat and was overflowing with students. Most of them I'd never seen before. But then I spotted Geena over on the other side of the room, and my whole body relaxed a little bit. With Geena there — and when wasn't she there? — detention couldn't be all bad. Right?

With all the students' eyes on me, I walked down the center of the room and handed my pink slip to the detention monitor. He'd been too absorbed in *Detention Weekly* magazine to even notice when I walked in the room. But he looked up when I told him my name.

"Addie Singer," I said, waiting for the inevitable.

"Singer?" He peered up at me, studying my face.

"Yes," I confirmed, rolling my eyes. It looked like even in detention I couldn't escape my brother's shadow. "Ben Singer's little sister."

"Hmm." The detention monitor shook his head and went back to his magazine. "Never heard of him."

Hey — finally something Ben hadn't done!

Anyway, it turned out that detention wasn't as bad as I thought — even though a whole week of it got kind of boring after a while. There's only so much staring into space you can do before you run out of things to think about. It did give me plenty of time to write some new songs, though. And when I got home from my last day of detention, I was feeling so good that I had to sing my favorite one, right away.

I grabbed my guitar from my bedroom and came down to the kitchen. I leaned back against the chair and started strumming my guitar — for the first time in a long time, I felt like I didn't have a care in the world. And it felt good.

Got my own legend. Got my own story.
Not waiting for Ben to hog all the glory.
It's finally my turn.
Yeah, it's my turn.
It's finally, it's finally my turn.

Ben walked through, talking to some girl on his cell phone. I waited for him to tell me to keep quiet, like he always does, but this time he just gave me a grin and leaned against the doorway, still chatting away.

"No, it's not the radio," he explained into the phone. "It's my sister. She's pretty good, actually. I wish I could play like that."

I almost choked — had I just heard Ben say that I was *good*? And that he wished he could be more like *me*? I pinched myself hard on the arm — nope, not dreaming. This was real, waking life, and my brother was actually giving me a compliment. He thought I was good at something — better than he was! Maybe my dreams of superstardom were not that far off.

"I'd write you songs," he continued, "but nothing rhymes with Heather." There was a pause. "Well, yeah, feather, I guess, but —" Another pause. "I guess weather, too. . . . Yeah, and tether. And together." He stopped talking again, clearly waiting for Heather to give him space to speak. Finally, he gave up. "Look, if you're gonna be like that, you can write your own songs."

Ben walked out of the kitchen, and I stared after him in disbelief, wondering if I'd just imagined the whole thing. But it had happened. It was unbelievable — I'd had something that was my own all along. . . . I just didn't realize it. So, I'll never be just like Ben. But that's okay, because he'll never be just like me.

Memo to self: Must make sure Ben never takes guitar lessons.

*   *   *

You might think that discovering my own unique talent was the best thing to come out of this whole mess. And okay, I'll admit that it's a *huge* relief to know that I have something that Ben never had, and never will. Something that I actually love — and I'm good at. I guess I realized that I don't have to work so hard at being something more than Ben Singer's little sister — because I *am* something more than that. So maybe I shouldn't have worried so hard. Sooner or later, people would have figured it out.

But I'm kind of glad it's sooner. And I'm almost glad it happened the way it did. Because discovering my own unique talent *wasn't* the only great thing to come out of this whole mess — I just didn't know it until a few days later. That's when I found out that things were about to get a whole lot better.

I was hanging out at *Juice!* with Geena and Zach, like always. And, like always, I was doing my best to ignore Ben, who was up at the counter flirting his heart out with some cute high school girl.

"Well hel-*lo*," he said as she bounced up to the counter. "You look like a Fantasmaberry . . . sixteen ounce?"

The girl batted her eyes at him, totally impressed. "How'd you know?"

Ben tried to look modest — and tried to look as if he hadn't made a list of what every pretty girl in school liked to order. "It's a gift."

I rolled my eyes and, like I said, tried to ignore him. Geena and Zach were way more interesting.

"I think your next column should be about turning health back into gym," Zach complained, patting his abs. "I'm starting to get soft."

Geena and I both stifled a laugh. Zach likes to think of himself with a ton of muscles, but he's about as thin as a flagpole and can probably lift about two pounds more than I can. On a good day. But Geena and I do our best to play along — after all, that's what best friends do.

"I don't think there's gonna be a next column." I sighed, changing the subject. Mary Ferry had banned me from the paper for "journalistic sloppiness" and once Mary Ferry made up her mind that was it.

"What?" Geena did a double take and almost spit out a mouthful of smoothie all over me. "That's crazy. You have a name to live up to."

"Forget it." I shook my head. I didn't feel like going into being fired by Mary Ferry with Geena and Zach. "I'm tired of living up to Ben's name."

"Not Ben's name," Geena corrected me. "Your own."

Up at the counter, the cute girl was staring at Ben, as if trying to figure something out.

"Wait a minute . . . I know you," she murmured.

Ben just shrugged. Of course she knew him, he probably figured — didn't everyone? Suddenly, it must have clicked, because the girl got a huge, excited grin.

"You're that girl's older brother!" she squealed.

Geena, Zach, and I whirled around — Ben's shocked expression matched my own.

"What's her name?" the girl continued, as Ben and I both gaped at her in disbelief. "Turdy Singer!"

As the girl burst into laughter, Ben narrowed his eyes at me, then leaped over the counter toward me. I jumped out of my seat and raced out of the café, with Ben closing in fast.

"Are you kidding!" he shouted, panting as he ran after me — he knew he needed to catch me before we got home. Probably figured I'd lock myself in my room until he was safely off at college. "Ten years of making a name for myself, and now I'm Turdy Singer's older brother?!"

As I raced home, I couldn't help smiling, even as the wind whipped past my face and my legs felt like they were about to fall off. Yes, once Ben caught me, he'd probably hang me upside down or stuff me down the laundry chute to punish me for ruining his reputation.

And yes, the whole school now knew me as "Turdy Singer"— a nickname that would probably only disappear once I'd done something else to publicly humiliate myself. But I'd accomplished my mission. I'd made a name for myself. Maybe it wasn't a great name — but it was mine, all mine.

And for the first time in my entire life, Ben was in *my* shadow. It looked like, from now on, thanks to me, the whole world would know him as Addie Singer's big brother.

Uh . . . I mean, *Turdy* Singer.

Okay, it's not perfect — but, hey, it's a start!

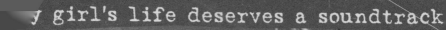
y girl's life deserves a soundtrack

and more

emma ★ roberts

Music from the hit TV show

10 TRACKS
performed by
Emma Roberts

Including
Punch Rocker
New Shoes
Mexican Wrestler

and her new hit
I Wanna Be